TEXAS JACK at the ALAMO

TEXAS JACK
at the ALAMO

Written and
Illustrated by James Rice

PELICAN PUBLISHING COMPANY
Gretna 1998

First printing, June 1989
Second printing, December 1998

Library of Congress Cataloging-in-Publication Data

Rice, James, 1934-
    Texas Jack at the Alamo / written and illustrated by James Rice.
        p. cm.
    Summary: An illustrated recounting of the battle of the Alamo in 1836,
as told from the perspective of a jackrabbit.
    ISBN 0-88289-725-X
    1. Alamo (San Antonio, Tex.)—Siege, 1836—Juvenile
literature.
    [1. Alamo (San Antonio, Tex.)—Siege, 1836.] I. Title.
    F390.R47 1989
    976.4′35103—dc19   88-31691
                                                                    CIP
                                                                     AC

Printed in Hong Kong
Published by Pelican Publishing Company, Inc.
1000 Burmaster Street, Gretna, Louisiana 70053

THE ALAMO

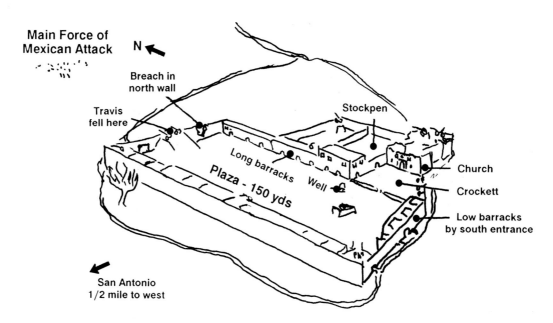

Introduction

The Texans had unofficially declared their independence from Mexico. After listening to the Texans' complaints, General Santa Anna set forth in late 1835 with the Mexican army to crush any resistance. As he started north, his first obstacle was the small town of San Antonio and a makeshift fort converted from an old church and manned by a mere handful of undisciplined defenders. The fort was named Alamo.

It was a cold late winter in 1836 and San Antonio wasn't much more than a sleepy little South Texas town. A few Texans were turning the old church a half-mile east of town into a regular fort.

The commander of the fort, young Bill Travis, ignored Jim Bowie's orders from General Sam Houston to destroy the place and leave.

Texas Jack sez the only way a body could lead Texans was to find out which direction they was agoin' and git out in front of them. They didn't take orders too good.

Horsemen rode into the fort in small groups from all directions. The most famous volunteer was Davy Crockett from Tennessee. Their numbers rose to 150.

Texas Jack sez that after ole Davy came with his fiddle and started them fandangos, the old church became the liveliest place around.

Dan Cloud, a Texan twenty-one years old, was a lookout in the tower of the San Fernando Church. He rang the bell when he saw Mexican riders coming in from the south. Colonel Travis was surprised. He didn't expect the soldiers for another month or so because of the cold weather.

Texas Jack sez them Mexican horse soldiers was duded up real pretty for fighting men.

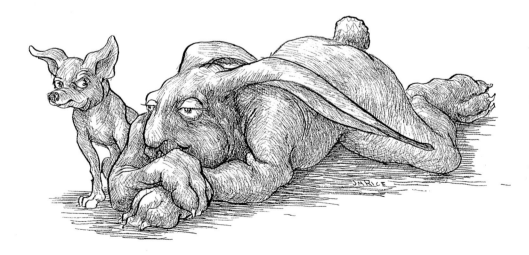

The sign on the food stand reads:

TORTILLOS
FRIJOL
TAMALE
CHILE
AGUA
CAFÉ

The first horsemen were followed by supply carts and then foot soldiers marching in long lines. The soldiers set up camps wherever they could find shelter. The Mexican leader was General Santa Anna, a hard, seasoned veteran of many battles.

Texas Jack sez there was shore something building up—he bet San Antone hadn't seen that much excitement in a month of Sundays.

Jim Bowie and Bill Travis both claimed leadership of the fort. The argument was settled when Bowie fell from a platform while helping install a cannon. He had serious injuries and his condition was complicated by pneumonia.

When Travis sent messengers for help at the Alamo, no one came. He found enough food but the ammunition supply was short.

Meanwhile Santa Anna's forces marched into the plaza in front of the San Fernando Church and the dragoons waved their long knives. It looked like the whole world was filling with Mexicans.

Texas Jack sez he never seen such show-offs.

Every day more Mexicans marched in. Davy Crockett was the best shot on either side. He often stood on the wall and fired at any soldier who showed himself. The Mexicans' short rifles were unable to hit "Kwoki," as they called him. They learned to run for cover when they saw him on the wall with his buckskins and long rifle.

Six men came from Santa Anna's camp to dam off the Texans' water supply. Texan sharpshooters got all six. It wouldn't have helped to have dammed the canal. The Texans had a well inside the fort.

Texas Jack sez he was glad nobody was taking potshots at jackrabbits that day.

The Mexican forces were nearing five thousand in number. Travis realized his situation was bad. Santa Anna sent a messenger to the fort with a white flag.

He offered to accept the Texans' surrender at "discretion," terms meaning probable execution by the captors. The Texans were not friendly.

Texas Jack sez that Mexican shore didn't waste a lot of time getting back to where he was out of range.

The Mexicans ran up a red flag on the tower of the San Fernando Church. Somebody back in their camp played a chilling tune on a trumpet—it was a deguello and it meant no quarter would be given the Texans.

The Mexicans kept up a round-the-clock bombardment with rifles and cannon. Every night under cover of darkness, the cannon were moved closer. The constant bombardment weakened the walls of the Alamo and kept the defenders from getting any rest.

Texas Jack sez it may not have harmed any bodies but it shore shattered everybody's nerves.

On the ninth day of the siege, James Bonham returned from Gonzales with thirty-two reinforcements. The Texans celebrated until 3 A.M.

Texas Jack sez things would've turned out different if more of them reinforcements Travis had sent for had showed up.

COME AND TAKE IT

On the next day, Travis allowed anyone to leave if he wished. Only one man, Louis Rose, a professional soldier, left. He said he did not come to the Alamo to die. He had proven in previous battles that he was no coward.

Texas Jack sez nobody even noticed when he crossed the line to stay.

Twice the Mexicans were beaten back, then on the third try they broke through a hole in the north wall near the area defended by Travis.

Texas Jack sez that's when he went to the south wall to help Davy.

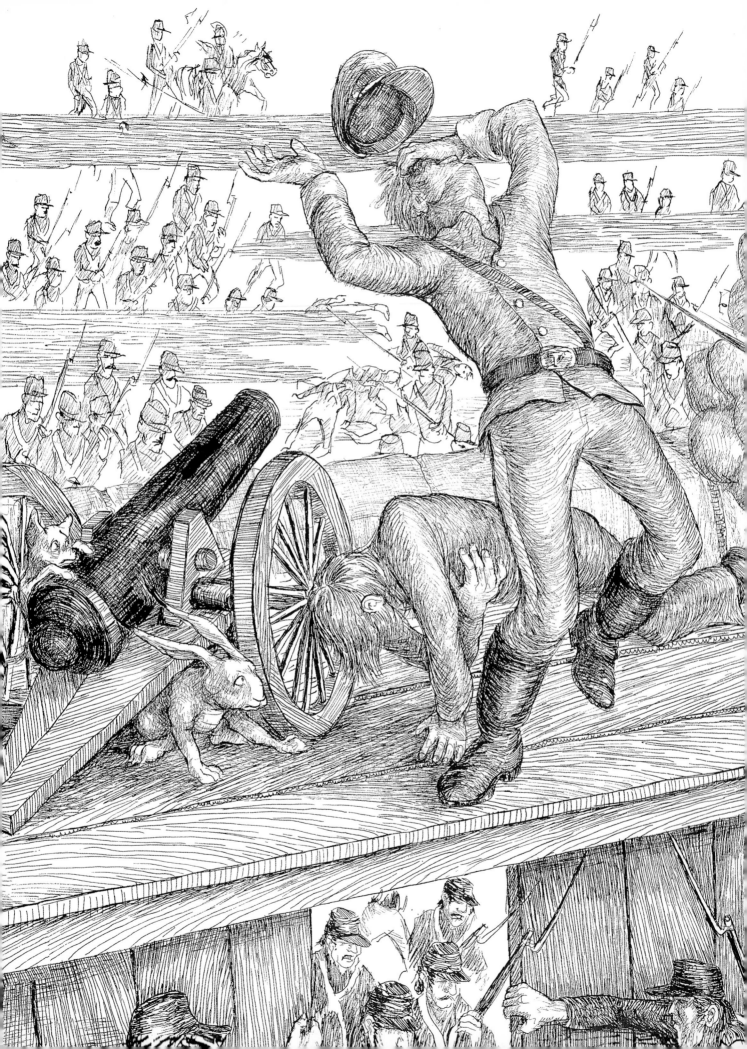

Travis was one of the first Texans killed. He was caught by a rifle ball between the eyes.

The Texans who had ammunition left didn't have time to reload as the attacking infantry poured through the breach.

Texas Jack sez he wished he could've helped more but he just couldn't handle them Texas long rifles.

Davy Crockett killed eight Mexicans and wounded
several more with his clubbed rifle before he was sur-
rounded and killed. Bowie fought from his sickbed in
the chapel until he was overcome.

The victors allowed no one to surrender.
It was over before 8 A.M.

Texas Jack sez he never in his whole life seen anything so awful happen in so short a time.

Fifteen civilians survived, including Mrs. Dickinson and her daughter, the only Anglos. The Mexicans lost 1,544 men. Of the Texans, 182 were killed, including 3 Mexicans and 14 whose identities weren't known.